MW01101290

LISTEN TO THE BUSH TALES SOUNDTRACK
AT WWW.BUSHTALES.COM

What Kind Of Elephant Are You?
This is a First Edition Book.

Published in 2010 by
Zorilla Entertainment Ltd,
Oak Cottage Studios,
Leigh On Mendip,
Somerset,
BA3 5QP

Printed in the UK by
Butler, Tanner & Dennis

ISBN 978-1-907430-00-8

www.bushtales.com

For the love of withered weasels!

ILLUSTRATIONS BY
FABRIZIO PETROSSI

COLOURING BY
VALERIA TURATI

ORIGINAL OIL PAINTING BY
KIRSTEN HARRIS

BUSH TALES

WHAT KIND OF ELEPHANT ARE YOU?

WRITTEN & CREATED BY

MATTHEW R JAMESON

Deep in the woods lived an elephant,
Not the romping, stomping, enormous sort,
But a prancing, dancing, happy go-lass,
Who was full of smiles and razzamatazz.
She would tender the flowers, plants and trees,
Keep the forest looking lush and green,
And help her friends as best she knew,
Everybody loved little **Dassie Pertu.**

One fine day
whilst elephant,
Was trying to pick
her favourite lunch,
A cheeky, squeaky,
trickster mouse,
Crept up and roared
like a mighty lion.

She leapt so high, she reached the sky,
And landed with a **thud** and **cry**,
'You could have scraped my trunk you fool!
What kind of **crazy mouse** are **you**?'

'But you're so **big** and I'm so small,
You shouldn't be afraid at all!
What kind of elephant are you?'
Said the cheeky mouse to Dassie Pertu.

But the **hullabaloo** had drawn a crowd
And all her friends were laughing out loud.
Upset and confused she wanted to cry,
So Dassie Pertu decided to fly.

Far, far away from the sniggers and jeers,

Saggy and sad and alone with her tears,

She collected her thoughts,

'I feel such a fool!

Maybe I'm not an elephant at all!'

From out of the trees **crashed** a matriarch queen,
All **trunk** and **tusks** and pure **elephanteen**.

As she **rumbled** on by she paused for a thought,
As her eye caught Pertu all slumped and forlorn.

'**W**hy do you have such a frown in your crown?
All that sniff'ling and sniv'ling, what's got you down?
I'm **wrinkled** and **crusty** but listening's my thing,
You can tell your troubles to **Ophelia Bing**.'

'I used to be such a happy-go girl,
'Til a wee cheeky squeak blew
the hair off my tail,
And now all my friends
think I'm stupid and daft,
What kind of elephant is **that?**
I hear them all laugh.'

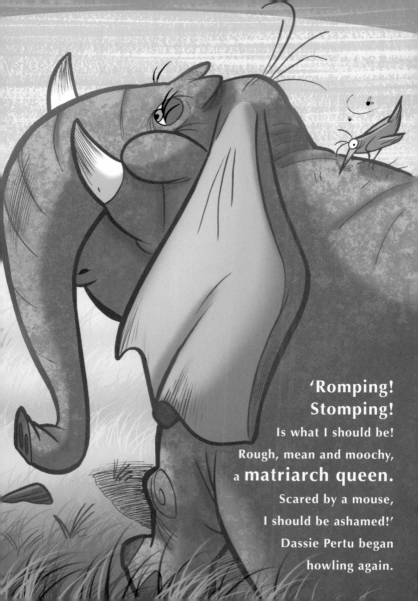

'Romping!
Stomping!
Is what I should be!
Rough, mean and moochy,
a **matriarch queen.**
Scared by a mouse,
I should be ashamed!'
Dassie Pertu began
howling again.

'If that's what **you** want,
then that's what **I'll** do!
In six **easy, easy** steps,
I'll make an elephant of **you!**'

'**S**teps **1** to **3** is all you need
to **scare** away your enemy.

You've got to,
blow your trunk,
flap your ears,
Stamp your feet,
and **show no fear!**'

'**O**nly a fool wouldn't step aside,
When an elephant makes an angry charge.
Have I given you a clue,
Of what an elephant would do?'

'Steps **4** to **6** is all you need,
To feast the prickly acacia tree.
Never **pluck** with the trunk
as you better beware,
To pick a pod or two
is a **thorny affair!**'

'**Tear** out a tree,
slam it on down,
Shake 'til the pods
have hit the ground.

Go ahead and try a few
It's what an elephant would do!'

'There's one more step at the end of the day,
When your **stresses** and **strains** need soaking away.'

'Breathe in all your worries
and spray out with love.
And dust away all that nonsense and blub.'

Dassie Pertu returned to the wood

and she romped and stomped

like an elephant should

She pulled up the flowers

and squashed the plants

Uprooted the trees and stripped the bark

She grumbled and rumbled, bellowed and 'blowed'

Scared all her friends and messed up the grove

'You're Wetched, a Wuffian, a Wogue and a Wascal, a Woughneck and Wude!'

Wailed a Withered old Weasel.

All Pertu's friends
were angry and mad,
'Behave or get out
you're destroying our land!'
'I'm a real elephant now!'
said Dassie Pertu.
'If that's what you want,
then that's what I'll do!
Out there on the plains
is where I should be.
Where the elephants roam,
elephants like me!'

Later that day whilst Dassie Pertu,

Was plucking a prickly acacia or two,

A growling snarl ro**ared** from behind,

Dassie just laughed,

'Why should I mind?

Go-away silly mouse,

I'm tired of your **tricks!**'

But Dassie Pertu was faced with a **fix!**

Masavi the lion
and his hungry pride,
Glared back at Pertu
with a drool and a smile.
These fang-dangled cats were no match for Pertu,
'Think oh think! What would a real elephant do?'
One step at a time is what she had learned,
But her head was all **muddled**
and **fuddled** with nerves.

The lions got closer
and **clink** went their claws.
Poor Dassie passed out,
she could take **no more!**

Brazen and brash, all muzzle and horns,
Charged Ophelia Bing and her **buffalo bulls.**

They **scuffled** and **brawled**,
scrapped and **scratched**,
The lions all fled,
they were **trampled**
and **smashed!**

'**Y**ou've had a lucky escape,' said Ophelia Bing.
'Messed up the forest and upset your friends.
Don't **ever** pretend to be an elephant like **me**.
You're different, that's all, and it's **meant to be!**'

'**I**'m Wetched and Wude!'
said a shame-faced Pertu.
'I should **never** have tried
to be an elephant like **you.**
Back in the forest
is where I should be,
Just being myself
and living the **dream!'**

Dassie Pertu returned to the woods,

And she danced and pranced as a happy-lass should.

She was full of smiles and a carefree stride,

And tendered the plants with a careful eye.

Never again did she leave her grove

Or behave like a Wascal, Wuffian or Wogue.

She lived in the forest as best she knew,

Everybody loved little **Dassie Pertu.**